# Snowflake and Sparkle

Rocky, the old ginger tomcat who lived next door, was perched on the fence. He looked disgusted. "A cat who thinks she's a dog!" Rocky meowed, staring at Sparkle as she chased the ball. "What is the world coming to?"

"Sparkle's my best friend," Snowflake woofed.

Rocky glared at him. "Cats and dogs aren't *meant* to be friends," he pointed out.

*Jenny Dale's Best Friends*

**Best ♥ Friends**

# Snowflake and Sparkle

### by Jenny Dale
### Illustrated by Susan Hellard

#### A Working Partners Book

Troll

To Mary and Louise Landri, with love

*Special thanks to Narinder Dhami*

Text copyright © 2002 by Working Partners Limited.

Illustrations copyright © 2002 by Susan Hellard.

*Best Friends* is a trademark of Working Partners Limited.

Published by Troll Communications L.L.C.

Reprinted by arrangement with Macmillan Children's Books, London.

ISBN 0-8167-7511-7

Printed in Canada.

10 9 8 7 6 5 4 3 2

## Chapter One

"Come on, Snowflake! Follow me!" Sparkle scampered off across the grass. She was chasing the soft, spongy ball that their owner, Ben, had just thrown for them. "Bet I get to the ball first!"

"Wait for me!" Snowflake barked at the speedy kitten. Sparkle's legs were much shorter than Snowflake's, but she always seemed to run much faster than he did. Snowflake was a creamy yellow golden retriever puppy. He had very soft fur and big, silky paws. Whenever he chased after things, his legs seemed to get tied up in knots.

"Got you!" Sparkle reached the ball and stopped it neatly with one white paw. But as she turned, she saw Snowflake pounding across the garden toward her. "Snowflake!" Sparkle meowed in alarm. "STOP! Look out for the holly bush!"

"Help!" Snowflake barked as he tried to skid to a halt. "Get out of my way, Sparkle!" His legs skittered in every direction as he slipped and slithered on the damp grass. Crunch! He landed headfirst in the prickly holly bush.

"Are you all right?" Sparkle meowed, rushing over to Snowflake as he picked his way out from among the spiky leaves.

"No, I scratched my nose," Snowflake whimpered, rubbing his muzzle with his paw.

Sparkle felt very sorry for her friend. "Bend down, and I'll give it a lick," she meowed. Reaching up on tiptoe, she gently licked Snowflake's sore nose.

"I think I'll just sit and watch from now on," Snowflake woofed. He flopped down onto the grass. "You're *so much* better at chasing things than I am, Sparkle."

"It's more fun if you're playing with me, though," Sparkle meowed, feeling disappointed. She picked up the squashy ball in her mouth and trotted back to Ben.

"Good job, Sparkle." Ben laughed. "You're more like a puppy than a kitten!"

Sparkle purred proudly. She loved chasing after things and bringing them back to Ben.

Snowflake watched as Ben threw the ball across the lawn again for Sparkle. He wished he was as clever as his friend. Sparkle never tripped or slipped or knocked things over, like Snowflake did.

Sparkle always moved quickly and neatly. She was a very pretty kitten, with thick tortoiseshell fur. She kept her little white bib and her four white paws very clean, even though she loved running around and playing in the garden.

"*Well!* I've never seen anything like *that* before!"

Snowflake jumped up, nearly tripping over his own paws. *Who said that?* He looked around.

Rocky, the old ginger tomcat who lived next door, was perched on the fence. He looked disgusted. "A cat who thinks she's a dog!" Rocky went on, staring at Sparkle as she chased the ball. "What is the world coming to?"

"Hello, Rocky," Snowflake woofed,

wagging his feathery tail. He was secretly rather scared of the grumpy old tomcat.

"It's just not right," Rocky grumbled. "You're the dog, so *you* should be chasing the ball and bringing it back." He stared rudely at Snowflake. "Don't you think it's odd?"

"Not at all!" Snowflake barked happily. "Sparkle's my *best* friend."

Rocky glared at him. "Cats and dogs aren't *meant* to be friends," he pointed out. "You should be barking and growling and chasing us." He bared his teeth at Snowflake. "Come on, chase me!"

Snowflake didn't want to chase Rocky. He'd seen the big cat standing up to other dogs on the street. They usually ran off howling, after Rocky had scratched them on the nose. "No, thank you," Snowflake woofed politely.

"In my day, cats were cats and dogs were dogs," Rocky went on grumpily.

"Well, I think Sparkle is *great*," Snowflake barked, sticking up for his friend. But the old tomcat just looked even more grumpy.

"Hello, Rocky." Sparkle trotted over to them. "Did you see me chase the ball?"

"Yes, I did!" Rocky spat. "You'd never catch *me* running after a ball like that!"

"Why not?" Sparkle was puzzled.

Rocky's whiskers twitched with anger. "Because I like being a cat, not a dog," he hissed. "Cats are good at different things, like climbing trees and jumping

off fences. We chase *mice*, not balls."
He looked down snootily at Snowflake.
"I could *never* be friends with a dog."

The ginger tomcat jumped down from
the fence into the neighbor's garden,
landing neatly on his paws. Then he
stalked off, the tip of his tail waving
angrily.

Sparkle stared at the fence where he'd
been sitting. "What a miserable old
puss!" the kitten meowed. "I'm glad he's
not *my* best friend!" And she nuzzled
Snowflake's ear.

"Look, Ben's throwing the ball for you
again," Snowflake barked.

"Come and play with us, Snowflake,"
purred Sparkle. Playfully, she nudged one
of his big, floppy paws with her pink

nose. "I promise I'll give you a chance to get the ball first."

But before the puppy could bark a reply, Sparkle suddenly froze. "Hold on a minute," she meowed. "I can hear someone opening *our* gate. Someone is coming up *our* front walk. Let's go see who it is!"

"Sparkle, come back here!" Snowflake woofed.

But the kitten wasn't listening. She ran over to the side gate and wriggled underneath it into the front yard. The visitor was a man in a blue jacket. He was carrying a bundle of letters.

"Aha!" Sparkle meowed. "I knew I'd heard someone!" She planted herself right in the middle of the front walk, blocking the man's way to the house.

The mailman didn't notice Sparkle at first because he was too busy sorting through the pile of letters in his hand. But then he looked up. His eyes nearly popped out of his head when he saw the kitten glaring at him.

"You're that person who pushes things through the mail slot every morning," Sparkle meowed fiercely. Her fur bristled all over as she eyed the mailman sternly. Sparkle knew that Ben's dad got really angry when he opened the envelopes marked "Bill." She bared her teeth at the mailman and hissed.

Just then the side gate swung open, and Ben and Snowflake came through.

"Sparkle, stop! You're frightening the

mailman!" Snowflake woofed.

"Well!" The mailman was scratching his head, looking dazed. "I've never been growled at by a *kitten* before. Dogs, yes. Cats, no."

Ben laughed. "Sparkle thinks she's a dog. And you know what, Sparkle? You're even more doggy than Snowflake is!" Ben ruffled his puppy's ears fondly.

Sparkle purred loudly, feeling very pleased with herself. "Did you hear that, Snowflake?" she meowed. "Ben thinks I'm more like a dog than you are. Maybe I should learn to bark!"

She opened her mouth as wide as she could, but all that came out was a great big MEOW.

"I think you'd better keep practicing!" Snowflake woofed, giving his friend a lick on the nose. "Maybe I can teach you."

"That would be great!" Sparkle purred as she ran through the side gate with Ben.

Ben turned. "Come on, Snowflake!" he called.

"Coming!" woofed Snowflake. But as he followed them, his tail drooped. He felt miserable. He couldn't help wishing that he could be more like Sparkle. He knew Ben loved him, but sometimes Snowflake didn't feel like a *real* dog at all.

## chapter Two

"Do you want to share some of this, Sparkle?" woofed Snowflake. He was sitting in his basket in the warm kitchen, chewing on a tasty biscuit. It was dinnertime, and he and Sparkle had been playing in the yard all afternoon.

"No, thanks." Sparkle's pink nose was twitching madly. "I can smell something *much* more exciting." And she stared up at Ben, who was sitting at the kitchen table eating his dinner. Sparkle knew exactly what it was. Tuna sandwiches!

Sparkle loved tuna. But Ben's mom didn't like Ben feeding Sparkle and Snowflake tidbits while he was eating. Sparkle fixed her big, green eyes on Ben. She simply had to get some of that delicious tuna. . . . Suddenly she had a brilliant idea.

With a loud meow, Sparkle lifted herself up on her back legs and sat down with her front paws in the air.

Snowflake stopped chewing his biscuit and stared. "What are you trying to do, Sparkle?" he woofed.

"Sit up and beg, like Ben tried to teach *you!*" Sparkle replied. She wobbled a bit at first, but then she got her balance.

Snowflake watched, his large brown eyes full of surprise. *He* hadn't managed

to sit up and beg yet. Every time he tried, he ended up rolling over onto his back.

"Ben!" Sparkle meowed proudly, and she patted her owner's leg with her paw. "Look at me!"

Ben glanced down. "Mom, look!" he cried. "Sparkle's learned to sit up and beg. Isn't she smart?" He laughed and slipped the kitten a little piece of tuna sandwich. Sparkle purred loudly as she munched it up.

Snowflake went back to chewing his biscuit. But somehow it didn't taste quite as good as it did before. Sparkle was *so* clever, he thought. Sometimes Snowflake wondered if Sparkle should have been a puppy—she was so much better at doggy things than he was. He would rather curl up in his basket and sleep than chase balls and beg for food.

"Can I share your basket, please?" Sparkle trotted over, yawning. "I think I might take a little nap."

"Yes, of course you can," Snowflake woofed, moving over to make room for the kitten. Sparkle had her own bed in the laundry room, but she preferred sharing Snowflake's. It was much cozier with two of them.

Sparkle climbed in and gave herself a good wash all over. Then she snuggled down and curled up against Snowflake's warm, soft tummy.

"You're so clever, Sparkle," Snowflake said. "I wish *I* could sit up and beg."

"I'll teach you." Sparkle yawned. "There's nothing to it. . . ."

But little by little, Sparkle's eyes began to close. And so did Snowflake's. The basket was near the radiator, and they were warm and cozy as they drifted off to sleep.

🐾 🐾 🐾

Sparkle woke up with a jump. She could hear the front door opening! She shot to her feet, blinking her green eyes, and leaped out of the basket. "Hold it right there!" she meowed fiercely.

"What's the matter?" Snowflake woofed sleepily. He'd been having a wonderful dream about burying a big, juicy bone.

"There's someone coming into the house." Sparkle ran over to the kitchen door, tail waving. "It better not be that man with the bills again. Or burglars. I'll chase them away in a hurry." She bared her teeth and tried to look scary.

Snowflake yawned. "It might be Ben's dad, coming home from work," he woofed. But Sparkle had already dashed off down the hall.

Snowflake rolled over on his back and stretched. They'd been asleep for a little while, and it was getting dark outside. The kitchen was empty. Ben and his mom were probably in the living room, watching the big box with the moving pictures.

Sparkle raced back in. "It *was* Ben's dad," she purred. "He says there's *snow* outside!"

"Snow!" Snowflake woofed, his tail beginning to wag madly. He jumped out of his basket, his paws skidding on the shiny floor.

"Yes, snow," Sparkle meowed, rubbing her head against Snowflake's front legs. "Isn't it great!"

"It's fantastic!" Snowflake agreed, giving the kitten a big lick on the nose.

They cocked their heads to one side and looked at each other.

"I don't know what *snow* is," Sparkle meowed at last. "Do you?"

"No." Snowflake's ears drooped. "But it sounds like my name."

"It must be something good," Sparkle decided, "because Ben's really excited.

I know! I'll look outside through my catflap."

The catflap was in the laundry room, next to the kitchen. Sparkle padded over to the door that led out into the backyard.

"Can I look too, Sparkle?" Snowflake barked politely. The kitten had told him lots of times that the catflap was for cats *only*.

"Well, all right," Sparkle agreed. "Just this once."

They peered through the clear window of the catflap. Their warm, furry bodies were pressed close together as they gazed outside. What they saw made their eyes open wide.

Enormous white flakes were swirling

down from the sky. They landed softly and thickly on the ground without making any noise at all. Everything in the yard was covered with a white coat that glittered in the moonlight. It looked like a different world.

"Wow!" woofed Snowflake quietly. "I wonder what snow *feels* like."

Sparkle stared longingly through the

catflap. "It looks soft, like the blanket in your basket, doesn't it? Let's go and find out!" She gave the catflap a push with her paw, but she wasn't strong enough yet to open it on her own. "Help me, Snowflake."

"I don't think I want to go outside," Snowflake whined. The snow looked beautiful, but it also looked wet and cold. He shivered in the icy draft that was blowing under the back door.

"Hey, what are you two doing?" Ben had popped his head around the doorway and spotted what the puppy and the kitten were up to. He came in and picked Sparkle up, then he carried her back into the kitchen.

Snowflake trotted after them.

"You can't go outside tonight," Ben went on, closing the door to the laundry room firmly. "It's much too cold. And, Sparkle, you can sleep in the kitchen with Snowflake. It's nice and warm in here."

"But I want to see the snow!" Sparkle yowled angrily as Ben put her gently in the basket and went out of the kitchen again.

"Maybe Ben will take us outside tomorrow," Snowflake woofed. He was quite happy to stay inside, all safe and warm.

"I don't want to wait till tomorrow," Sparkle whimpered, clawing impatiently at the blanket. "I want to see the snow NOW!"

"Go to sleep, Sparkle." Snowflake yawned.

"I can't go to sleep!" Sparkle meowed. "I'm much too excited." But she curled up next to Snowflake anyway.

Snowflake dozed off, dreaming of soft clouds of snow.

## Chapter Three

Snowflake had been fast asleep, but suddenly he woke up with a jump.

The house was silent and dark. Ben and his mom and dad must have gone to bed, he decided.

He shivered. The kitchen felt cold, which was strange. It usually stayed warm and cozy all night. Suddenly Snowflake realized that Sparkle wasn't curled up in the basket next to him.

"Sparkle?" Snowflake woofed quietly. He didn't want to wake up Ben and his mom and dad. "Where are you?"

There was no answer. Snowflake sat up and looked around the kitchen for his friend. Although it was nighttime, the pale moonlight shining in the window made it easy to see. But there was no sign of Sparkle.

Snowflake began to feel worried. Where *had* the kitten gone? Snowflake flattened his ears and whined as he remembered what Sparkle had said. *I want to go out and see the snow.* Snowflake hadn't really paid much attention at the time. After all, there was no way Sparkle could get outside.

Snowflake looked at the laundry room door. It was still closed. And so was the kitchen door. So Sparkle had to be in the kitchen *somewhere*.

"Maybe I should go and wake Ben up," Snowflake thought. But Ben would be mad if he thought that Sparkle had gone out in the snow. Sparkle would get into trouble.

"I know!" Snowflake leaped eagerly out of his basket. "I'll find Sparkle myself, just like a *real* dog would!"

He began to sniff the kitchen floor. Carefully he sniffed all around the basket, trying to figure out which way Sparkle had gone. There were lots of Sparkle smells around, but Snowflake was looking for the newest and strongest smell.

He found it! His black nose to the floor, Snowflake set off across the kitchen. He followed the trail right across the room,

until—BUMP! Snowflake was so busy sniffing, he banged into the cabinet under the sink.

"Ouch!" Snowflake sat down. He was confused. Surely Sparkle wasn't *inside* the cabinet? No, she wasn't tall enough to open the door. So where was she?

Snowflake snuffled around the bottom of the cabinet and around the vegetable cart next to it. But he couldn't tell which way Sparkle had gone.

"Sparkle, where *are* you?" Snowflake whimpered. He was shivering all over. The kitchen was freezing, and it seemed to be getting colder every minute.

Snowflake lifted his head. He sniffed hard, his nose twitching. He could smell crisp, frosty air coming from outside—as if someone had left the window open.

Snowflake stood up on his back legs and rested his front paws on the cabinet. He could see the window over the sink— and it *was* open, just a little. Snowflake had heard Ben's mom saying that the lock didn't work properly. Ben's dad had promised to fix it, but he hadn't gotten around to it yet.

Snowflake stared at the open window. Snow had settled on the windowsill, and he could just make out some tiny paw prints. The kitten must have climbed up the vegetable cart, onto the sink, and then wriggled out of the window!

Snowflake was tired and cold. He longed to climb into his basket, snuggle under his blanket, and go back to sleep. But he was too worried about Sparkle. What was happening to her, out there alone, in the deep snow?

"I'll just have to go into the yard and look for Sparkle myself," Snowflake woofed firmly. "But how I am going to get out?"

The puppy put his paw on the vegetable cart. It started to tip over.

Suddenly it shot away from him on its little wheels and crashed onto its side. Potatoes and carrots spilled out and tumbled across the floor.

Snowflake yelped and jumped away from the bouncing vegetables. "Well, I can't climb up that way," he thought. "And I can't jump high enough to get onto the sink. I'll have to find another way out!"

# chapter four

Snowflake sat down on the kitchen floor and scratched his ear while he thought about it. "There's only one way I can get outside," he decided. "I'll have to squeeze through Sparkle's catflap!"

This wasn't going to be easy. Snowflake looked at the laundry room door. It was firmly shut. He had to open it to reach the catflap in the back door. But how?

Snowflake knew how the door opened. He'd seen Ben do it lots of times. You pushed down on the silver handle, and then the door swung open. Snowflake trotted over to the door and gazed at it. He stood on his back legs and stretched his paw up to the handle. But he couldn't quite reach it.

"I'll have to *jump* up," he thought. "But I'm no good at jumping!"

He had to try, though. For Sparkle . . .

Snowflake jumped up into the air as high as he could. But he missed the handle completely and landed on the floor with a soft thud.

"Try again," Snowflake woofed to himself. So he did. But he missed it again.

"Grrr!" Snowflake was getting angry. He bared his teeth and glared at the door. "Let me out!"

He fixed his eyes on the door and

leaped into the air once more. This time
Snowflake's paw hit the handle hard.
The door swung open.

"I did it!" Snowflake barked excitedly.
Then he remembered that Ben and his
mom and dad were asleep upstairs.

He hurried over to the catflap. He

pushed it with his paw, and he was pleased when it swung outward. "*Sparkle* can't open the flap on her own," Snowflake thought proudly, "but I can!"

Snowflake nudged it open with his nose, like he'd seen Rocky doing next door. He stuck his head through and looked outside. The snow had almost stopped falling. There were just a few flakes still drifting down. The night air was freezing, and it made his ears tingle. But Snowflake wasn't giving up now.

He still felt a bit nervous about using the catflap, though. After all, it was supposed to be for *cats*, as Sparkle kept telling him. "But Sparkle behaves like a dog most of the time!" Snowflake woofed quietly to himself. "So why can't I pretend to be a *cat* just this once?"

Snowflake began to push through the flap. It was a tight fit, but Snowflake made it. "I did it!" he panted as he wriggled his back legs out. "I did it! *Oh!*"

He flopped through the catflap—and landed in a deep snowdrift. Only his nose and tail were left sticking out.

"Help!" Snowflake yelped. The snow

felt very strange. It was soft, like his blanket. But it was crisp and crunchy too, like one of his biscuits!

He scrambled out and shook himself. He was wet and cold, but the snow was fun. It was so soft and fluffy that it was really easy to dig. Snowflake wanted to dig a big hole, but he didn't have time. He had to find Sparkle.

He looked around and spotted a clear trail of kitten paw prints. They led away from the kitchen window, down to the garden. "This is easy!" Snowflake woofed. "All I have to do is follow the trail!"

Snowflake set off. The paw prints went down one side of the garden and back up the other, ending at the side gate near the house. The gap underneath the wooden gate was blocked with snow. But Snowflake could see that a small hole had been dug away in the middle.

He felt very worried. Ben didn't like them going into the front yard without him, because of the traffic in the street. He just hoped Sparkle was all right.

Snowflake had to dig a bigger hole with his front paws before he could squeeze under the gate. Then he set off again, following Sparkle's trail. Down the path, through the open gate, along the street, into the front yard of the house next door, and up to *their* side gate.

"I'm glad I didn't eat too many biscuits yesterday!" Snowflake thought, wriggling through the iron bars of the gate.

The paw prints went on, down to the

end of the yard next door. His nose to the ground, Snowflake followed them across the snowy lawn, until—

"OOPS!" Snowflake stopped at the edge of a small pond. At least, Snowflake *thought* it was a pond. But the water looked all wrong. It was white and shiny and *hard*. And it was dusted with glittering snow.

Snowflake put out his paw and tapped on the pond. It felt very slippery and it creaked a bit. Snowflake didn't think it was safe to walk on. But he could see that Sparkle *had* walked across it. There were tiny kitten paw prints leading right into the middle of the pond, where there was a big jagged hole. Snowflake could see the dark water underneath.

He suddenly felt very scared. Had Sparkle fallen into the pond?

A noise from behind him made Snowflake jump. He turned around and saw Rocky climbing out of his catflap.

"Hey!" The ginger tomcat looked furious when he spotted the puppy. "What are you doing in *my* yard?" He hissed and arched his back. "You'd better get out of here!"

"No, I won't!" Snowflake growled. He was so worried about Sparkle, he forgot how fierce Rocky could be. "I'm looking for my best friend, and you're not going to stop me!" And Snowflake snarled at him, showing all his teeth. The hair stood up on the back of his neck.

Rocky was so shocked, he turned around and dived back through his catflap. It slammed shut behind him, nearly nipping his tail.

Snowflake hurried back to the pond. To his relief, he saw the little paw prints began again on the other side of the hole. Sparkle must have managed to climb out of the water.

Snowflake set off again, nose to the ground. Sparkle's trail went right to the bottom of the yard and through a gap in the fence. Snowflake squeezed through too. Then, to his surprise, he saw *another* set of paw prints in the snow. They were a lot bigger than Sparkle's. "I wonder what kind of animal *that* is?" Snowflake woofed. He lifted his head and looked around.

He realized he was back in his own yard. He had found his *own* paw prints! They were the ones he'd made earlier, when he'd followed Sparkle's trail across their lawn.

Snowflake shivered miserably.

He was right back where he'd started.

And there was still no sign of Sparkle.

## chapter five

Snowflake didn't know *what* to do next. He was cold and tired, and Sparkle was nowhere to be seen. "Oh, Sparkle," he whimpered softly. "Where *are* you?"

*What was that?* Snowflake thought he'd heard a faint meow.

"*Meow!*"

There it was again, a bit louder this time. Snowflake looked around eagerly. His tail began to wag. "Is that you, Sparkle?" he barked. "Where are you?"

"I'm up here!" yowled a very miserable kitten voice.

Snowflake looked up. There, in the bottom branches of a tall tree, sat a wet and unhappy Sparkle.

"*Sparkle!*" Snowflake bounded over to the tree, his tail almost wagging right off. "I've been so worried about you! Why are you up *there?*"

"I was trying to get away from Rocky," Sparkle explained, shivering. "He chased me out of his yard, and he scratched my ear!"

"The big bully!" Snowflake growled. "Don't worry, Sparkle. I chased *him* away!"

"And I fell into the pond and got wet," Sparkle wailed. "I can't get back into the

house because I can't reach the window. And I can't open the catflap on my own."

"I can open the catflap for you," Snowflake woofed. "You need to go inside and warm up."

"But I don't think I can get down from this tree!" Sparkle meowed. "I'm scared I'll fall."

"I'll help you." Snowflake looked up at the kitten. "Put your paw on that branch just below you."

Sparkle did as she was told. She wobbled, but she didn't fall. Step by step, she began to make her way slowly down the tree. Snowflake watched anxiously. As soon as Sparkle jumped down onto the snow-covered lawn, he rushed over to her.

"Oh, I'm freezing!" Sparkle meowed, pressing herself up against her friend's warm, furry body. "I *hate* the snow!" She let Snowflake give her a few quick licks to warm her up. Then they set off along the garden path to the back door. The kitten couldn't wait to get out of the freezing cold and be warm and dry again.

"Jump inside," Snowflake told Sparkle, pushing the catflap open with his paw.

"I'm so glad *you* can open the catflap, Snowflake," Sparkle meowed weakly as she climbed in.

"Well, I won't use it again," Snowflake woofed. He hoped Sparkle didn't mind him using her catflap just this once. "I know it's for cats, really!"

Sparkle wasn't listening. She rushed

gratefully into the kitchen and over to the puppy's basket.

Snowflake picked up the blanket with his teeth so that Sparkle could creep underneath it. Then he curled up next to her.

"You feel all nice and cuddly and warm, Snowflake," Sparkle meowed sleepily. "I'm *so* glad to be home again."

## chapter Six

Sparkle stirred and snuggled deeper into the blanket. She didn't want to wake up yet, but she could feel something tickling her nose. . . .

Slowly she opened her eyes. Snowflake was next to her, licking her nose with his big pink tongue.

"It's time to wake up, Sparkle," Snowflake woofed. "Do you want to go out and play?"

Sparkle yawned. She was warm and

cozy in the basket, and she didn't feel like getting up. "No, I'm still sleepy," she meowed.

As Snowflake got out of the basket, Sparkle opened her eyes again and meowed, "Thank you, Snowflake."

"What for?" Snowflake barked.

"For coming to look for me last night, of course," Sparkle purred, rubbing her head against Snowflake lovingly. "You're my *very* best friend!"

"I didn't do much," Snowflake woofed.

"You *did!*" Sparkle meowed. "I was cold and wet and stuck up in that tree, and you found me and brought me home. *And* you chased Rocky away. I think you're the bravest, most brilliant dog in the whole world!"

Snowflake felt so proud. He decided that maybe he *was* a real dog after all!

It was snowing again. Snowflake hoped that Ben would take them outside to play when he'd finished his breakfast. He liked the snow. And he didn't even care if he saw Rocky again. Snowflake wasn't scared of the ginger tomcat anymore. He'd show him who was the *real* dog in Ben's house!

Just then the doorbell rang. To Snowflake's surprise, Sparkle didn't dash out to see who it was, like she always did. Instead she snuggled down in the basket again.

"Aren't you going to see who that is?" Snowflake barked.

"No, thank you," Sparkle meowed,

staying firmly where she was. "It's too cold!"

"Oh." Snowflake jumped to his feet and followed Ben out of the room. "Maybe *I'd* better go and see, then."

A big blast of freezing air rushed into the kitchen as Ben opened the front door.

Sparkle shivered and cuddled down farther under her blanket. She began to lick her paws, which were very dirty after her adventure.

"It was the mailman," Snowflake woofed as he bounded back into the kitchen. "He had a package for Ben's dad. I growled at him, just to show him who's in charge!"

"Mom, can I go out to play in the snow?" asked Ben, handing the package to his dad. "And can I take Snowflake and Sparkle with me?"

"What?" Sparkle yowled. "No way! I don't like getting cold and wet!" And she crawled even farther under the blanket, until only the tip of her tail was sticking out.

"I'll play with you, Ben!" Snowflake

eagerly raced over to the back door, wagging his tail. "Let's dig a big hole!"

When Snowflake and Ben had gone outside, Sparkle climbed carefully up onto the kitchen windowsill to watch them.

Snowflake was having a great time, racing around and digging in the snow, but Sparkle was glad to be safe and warm inside the house.

Snowflake saw his best friend watching through the window, and he wagged his tail at her.

"You know what, Sparkle?" he woofed. "It's great being a dog!"

"And you know what, Snowflake?" meowed Sparkle happily. "It's even better being a dog's best friend!"